W9-BTR-194

Signed, Abiah Rose

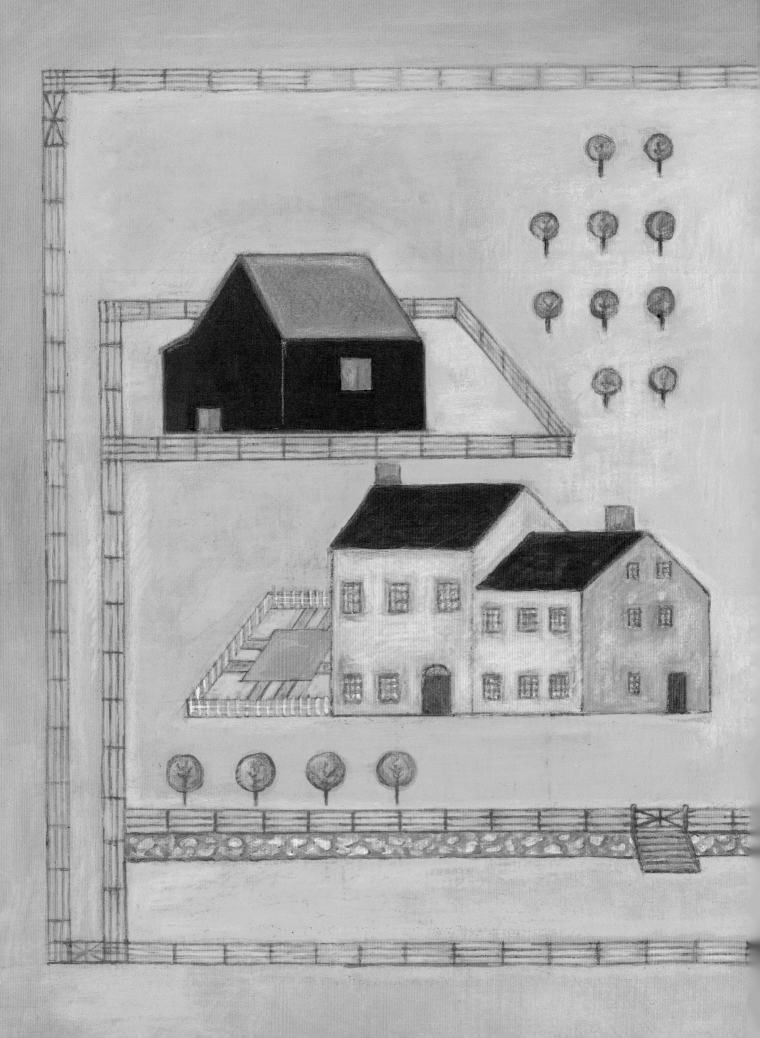

Signed,
Abiah Rose

WRITTEN & ILLUSTRATED BY
DIANE BROWNING

TRICYCLE PRESS
Berkeley

Terms Used in This Book

Calamanco—a glossy, woolen fabric.

Female academy—a school for girls.

Fireboard—the protective screen for a fireplace, often ornamental.

Floorcloth—a hand-painted canvas floor covering.

Keeping room—the sitting room reserved for family.

Limner—a painter, usually of portraits.

Mantle—a loose, sleeveless garment worn over other clothing.

Peddler—a traveling salesman.

Philadelphia pianoforte—the American version of the "square piano," which, in actuality, had a long, rectangular shape.

Wares—items for sale.

Whitewash—a paint made from a mixture of lime and chalk, used for whitening walls and fences.

Dedicated
to my artist sisters,
Janna and Barbara
&
in memory of my artist mother
Dorothy Browning,
whose work was never signed

My papa has a farm in the valley of
the Genesee River. We four children
have our own tasks to do about the
farm, but we each have our own talents
as well. My brother Eliah can whittle a
piece of wood until it is the very image
of a dog or a goose or a cat. Sister
Jerusha plays a Philadelphia pianoforte
and sings like a little bird. The youngest,
Katherine, stitches snips of calamanco
together with silk thread to make
wondrous quilts.

And I make pictures.

When I was very small I would smear soot from the hearth into the shapes of birds and flowers. Nurse said "no" and "dirty" and swept them away. I think I did not heed her overmuch.

When I was older, I wound papa's wagon 'round with leafy tendrils of painted vines. Papa was not pleased, though I heard him tell Mama that the vines looked real enough.

One bright May morning I could not help it. The desire to do something with my own hands overcame me, and I took the whitewash bucket to the new-painted barn.

It was much improved, I thought, with likenesses of our cow Delia
and our horse Becky, but Papa did not like it. This time he said, "Get
her some proper paints and a surface besides my barn and wagon upon
which to make her pictures."

Once I was supplied with colors and board, I painted my Papa's portrait in thanks. He must have liked it well enough, for he hung it in the keeping room. Mama asked could I paint Cousin Mariah's likeness for her ninetieth birthday. Papa said, "Best not. Serious painting is not girl's work." But he did show his portrait to our neighbor Mr. Prior who asked would I paint his also. As did our neighbor Mr. Pinney.

Before long, I had not only painted Mr. Prior and Mr. Pinney but every member of my family, the hired man, and his dog, Ira, too. So I set about looking for new subjects.

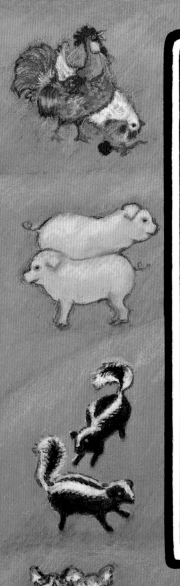

Now our Aunt Eliza can tell a tale better than anyone I know. When Eliah, Jerusha, Katherine, and I were children, we would gather about her every Sunday after supper and listen while Noah built his Ark to save himself and the creatures of the world from the Great Flood. And when the ladies of old Egypt pulled little baby Moses from the River Nile, we always exclaimed and sighed with relief.

Listening to Aunt Eliza, I felt I could almost touch the blue of Mary's mantle and the jig-jog patchwork of Joseph's coat. I wanted to make pictures as vivid as Aunt Eliza's stories.

I showed Mama my painting *Flight into Egypt* and she asked Papa if perhaps Pastor Winslow would like it for the church. "Best not," he said. But Pastor Winslow heard about *Flight* and greatly admired the painting when he came for a visit. So Papa gave it to him.

I asked if I should sign my name to *Flight*, but Mama cautioned me against being prideful. So instead, I began making my own mark upon my pictures: a tiny rose. I could hide it amongst the flowers or leaves or in the folds of a lady's skirt. It would be a secret thing, not my name really, so I saw no harm in it.

This summer, Uncle Albion came to visit. Uncle is a peddler, though he does not often come so far north as our valley. His colorful wagon, adorned with strings of spoons that joggle in the breeze, is a welcome sight to the folk of the Genesee.

I always think of it as a magic wagon, crammed full with all manner of things, from snips of ribbon to bolts of silk. It holds hammers and saws and nails and seeds and tiny bottles of syrup to cure all that ails.

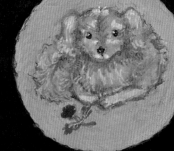

Once Uncle was fed and sat resting on our porch, I asked him if I might repaint his marvelous wagon with subjects of his own choosing.

"What is this!" he exclaimed, and insisted he see all my work, which he praised heartily. So I was allowed to paint Uncle's wagon, entertained all the while by tales of his travels. He told me of artists he knew who were all men, and old, but he declared I painted better than a fair number of them.

Uncle Albion's enthusiasm for my work inspired him to ask my parents if I might join him in his travels. He was very persuasive and after much discussion Papa said, "You may spend the summer helping your uncle. If a picture is requested, you may paint it, but the coins are to go to Albion for your keep. If there is more beyond his share, it shall go for your future life when you marry."

So, Uncle Albion and I set off to
travel the dusty roads of our wide,
green valley, offering our bolts of
yardage and cards of needles, and
visiting, too, with the farmers and
villagers along the way.

Uncle always knew where we would
be welcomed to stay the night or
to share a meal. We set my Bible
pictures about those dusty yards, and
housewives oohed and aahed and
offered us cold glasses of buttermilk
or apple cider.

"Stay till my husband can see these," they said.

"Just look at the blue of Mary's robe!"

"See the smile on the Babe's face!" And often they would buy one, or the farmer must have his wife painted with the children, or a portrait must be done of a baby son with his rattle of coral and bells.

Once I asked Uncle, "Shall I sign my name?" He smiled kindly and said, "Best not," and patted my shoulder. "'Tis good work, but will be appreciated more if you don't sign it, child. All the famous painters are men. A female painter's work will never be as highly valued. Be content with a job well done, and do not look for fame in this life, my girl."

So I continued to mark my pictures with a tiny rose instead.

One morning when I had set up my easel by the Genesee River, a
man with a pack on his back approached on foot. He was one of the
artists Uncle had told me of, a Mr. Sprigg. A sign painter in winter,
he closed up shop in summer to travel with his dog, Hiram, and paint
portraits and landscapes. He showed me his latest painting, which I
greatly admired. We spent hours discussing the mixing of colors and
various ways of capturing the light on the river. It was a wonderful day.

Now it is summer's end and I have returned to the farm. I presented my river painting to Papa and Mama, and everyone was full of questions about my travels.

But I have not told them yet that I have come home with a new idea. After supper tonight I will ask Papa if I may go live with his brother Ezra, who has a shop in town.

Uncle Ezra is a merchant like Uncle Albion, although he is not a bit like him otherwise. Uncle Ezra's wares are neatly arranged, and soberly sold off of shelves and out of long cases with glass covers. He has a small back room where I can paint portraits, signs, fireboards, and floorcloths year-round, and then sell them in the shop. If Papa's answer is, "Best not, Abiah Rose," I am determined to persist until he consents.

And when one day I do have my own shop in town, it will have a formal greeting area, a posing area with a painted backcloth, and comfortable chairs for people to sit upon as I paint their likenesses. I shall have cupboards full of colors and boards to paint upon and brushes from tiny to fat.

I believe, too, that by then Papa and Mama will agree that I might sign my name to my pictures and be anonymous no longer.

While I have been content with the coin and whatever appreciation I receive for my labors, I see no virtue in being unknown and no fault in the signing of my own girl's name upon the work of my own girl's hands.

Signed, *Abiah Rose*

# Author's Note

In eighteenth- and nineteenth-century America, before the camera was in widespread use, folk artists traveled from town to town selling portraits and landscapes. They were welcomed by farmers and townspeople who wanted to have likenesses painted of themselves, their families, and their homes. These were remembrances to pass down to their children, just as today we have photographic records of our own lives.

Both men and women artists sometimes signed their work, but it was the work, not the artist's name, that was important. A large number of those early paintings were done anonymously. Some art historians believe that many of the unsigned pieces may have been created by women.

At that time, a woman was expected to marry and run a household. Young girls were taught the decorative and useful arts, either by family members or in female academies. Most of their creative work was done for the adornment of their homes and had some practical function: samplers developed needle skills; quilts kept the family warm; embroidery decorated tablecloths, napkins, and handkerchiefs; paintings brightened walls. A young woman who began by painting or drawing family members might gain a local reputation as an artist. She could then supplement family finances by selling her work or teaching painting and drawing to young ladies. There were women who traveled the countryside as male artists did, and stayed at the home of customers while creating portraits of family members, but due to the independent nature of this lifestyle, these traveling women artists were few and far between.

Art history books have traditionally neglected the work of female artists. I was not aware of the rich contributions of women to pre-twentieth century American art until I saw Mirra Bank's PBS documentary *Anonymous Was a Woman* and its accompanying book. They revealed and explored the work of female folk artists, showing it to be as accomplished and creative as that of their male counterparts. This inspired me to imagine the heroine of *Signed, Abiah Rose* who, proud of her work, wanted to be recognized as an individual equal to her peers.

Can You Find Abiah's Roses?

Beginning with her biblical paintings, Abiah Rose hid a small red rose in each of her paintings. Can you find each one?

For Further Reading:

Bank, Mirra. *Anonymous Was a Woman*. New York: St. Martin's Press, 1995.

Dewhurst, Kurt, Betty MacDowell, and Marsha MacDowell. *Artists in Aprons: Folk Art by American Women*. New York: E.P. Dutton, 1979.

Fisher, L. E. *The Limners: America's Earliest Portrait Painters*. Tarrytown: Marshall Cavendish, 2000.

Panchyk, Richard. *American Folk Art for Kids: With 21 Activities*. Chicago: Chicago Review Press, 2004.

Heartfelt thanks to my amazing sister, Barbara Browning,
and my wonderful editor, Abigail Samoun.

Published in the United States by Ten Speed Press, an imprint of
the Crown Publishing Group, a division of Random House, Inc., New York.
www.crownpublishing.com
www.tricyclepress.com

Tricycle Press and the Tricycle Press colophon are registered trademarks of Random House, Inc.

Library of Congress Cataloging-in-Publication Data
Browning, Diane.
Signed, Abiah Rose / written and illustrated by Diane Browning. — 1st ed.
p. cm.
Summary: In pioneer days, a young girl who is a talented artist is
encouraged to paint portraits, Bible scenes, and other pictures, but told
never to sign her work, either because it would be a sign of pride or
because artists are expected to be men.
[1. Artists—Fiction. 2. Frontier and pioneer life—Fiction. 3. Sex
role—Fiction.] I. Title.
PZ7.B822182Sig 2010
[E]—dc22
2009022172

ISBN 978-1-58246-311-7 (hardcover)
ISBN 978-1-58246-347-6 (Gibraltar lib. bdg.)
Printed in Malaysia

Design by Katy Brown
Typeset in Adobe Caslon, Bromwich, Morris Golden, and Ovidius.
The illustrations in this book were rendered in acrylic and colored pencil.

1 2 3 4 5 6 — 15 14 13 12 11 10

First Edition